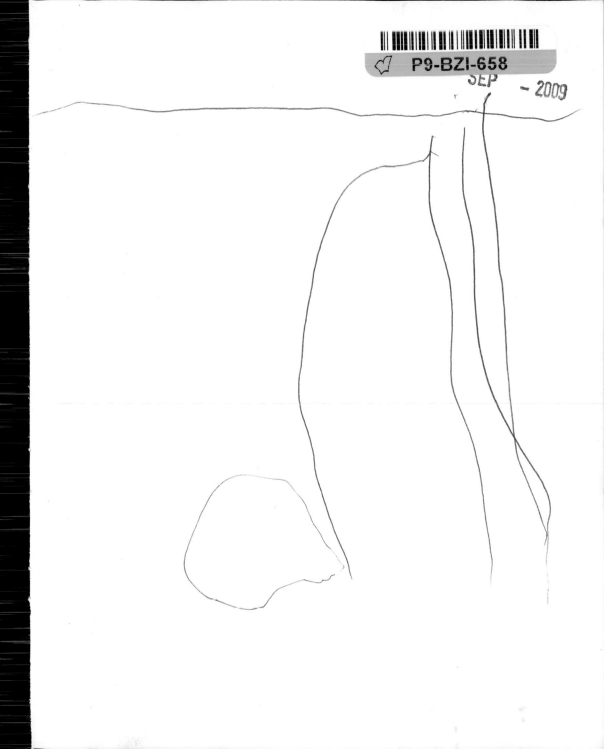

It's Fall, Dear Dragon

by Margaret Hillert

Illustrated by David Schimmell

NORWOOD HOUSE PRESS

DEAR CAREGIVER, The *Beginning-to-Read* series is a carefully written collection of classic readers you may remember from your own childhood. Each book features text comprised of common sight words to provide your child ample practice reading the words that appear most frequently in written text. The many additional details in the pictures enhance the story and offer the opportunity for you to help your child expand oral language and develop comprehension.

Begin by reading the story to your child, followed by letting him or her read familiar words and soon your child will be able to read the story independently. At each step of the way, be sure to praise your reader's efforts to build his or her confidence as an independent reader. Discuss the pictures and encourage your child to make connections between the story and his or her own life. At the end of the story, you will find reading activities and a word list that will help your child practice and strengthen beginning reading skills.

Above all, the most important part of the reading experience is to have fun and enjoy it!

Shannon Cannon

Shannon Cannon,
Literacy Consultant

Norwood House Press • P.O. Box 316598 • Chicago, Illinois 60631
For more information about Norwood House Press please visit our website at
www.norwoodhousepress.com or call 866-565-2900.

Text copyright ©2010 by Margaret Hillert. Illustrations and cover design copyright ©2010 by Norwood House Press, Inc. All rights reserved. No part of this book may be reproduced or utilized in any form or by any means without written permission from the publisher.

LIBRARY OF CONGRESS CATALOGING-IN-PUBLICATION DATA

Hillert, Margaret.
  It's fall, dear dragon / by Margaret Hillert ; illustrated by David Schimmell.
    p. cm. — (A beginning-to-read book)
Summary: "A boy meets his pet dragon after school to rake and jump in leaves, carve a pumpkin, and enjoy a pretty fall day"--Provided by publisher.
  ISBN-13: 978-1-59953-311-7 (lib. ed. : alk. paper)
  ISBN-10: 1-59953-311-1 (lib. ed. : alk. paper) [1. Dragons--Fiction. 2. Autumn--Fiction.] I. Schimmell, David, ill. II. Title. III. Title: It is fall, dear Dragon.
  PZ7.H558Isf 2009
  [E]--dc22

2009003883

Manufactured in the United States of America.

I have to go to school.
You cannot come with me.
I will come out.

It is good to be here
with friends.
I like school.

Aa Bb Cc Dd

Homework

English pg. 71-74

Math pg 42- 44

Spellino pg 50-51

Here I am.
Come with me now.
We can run and jump.

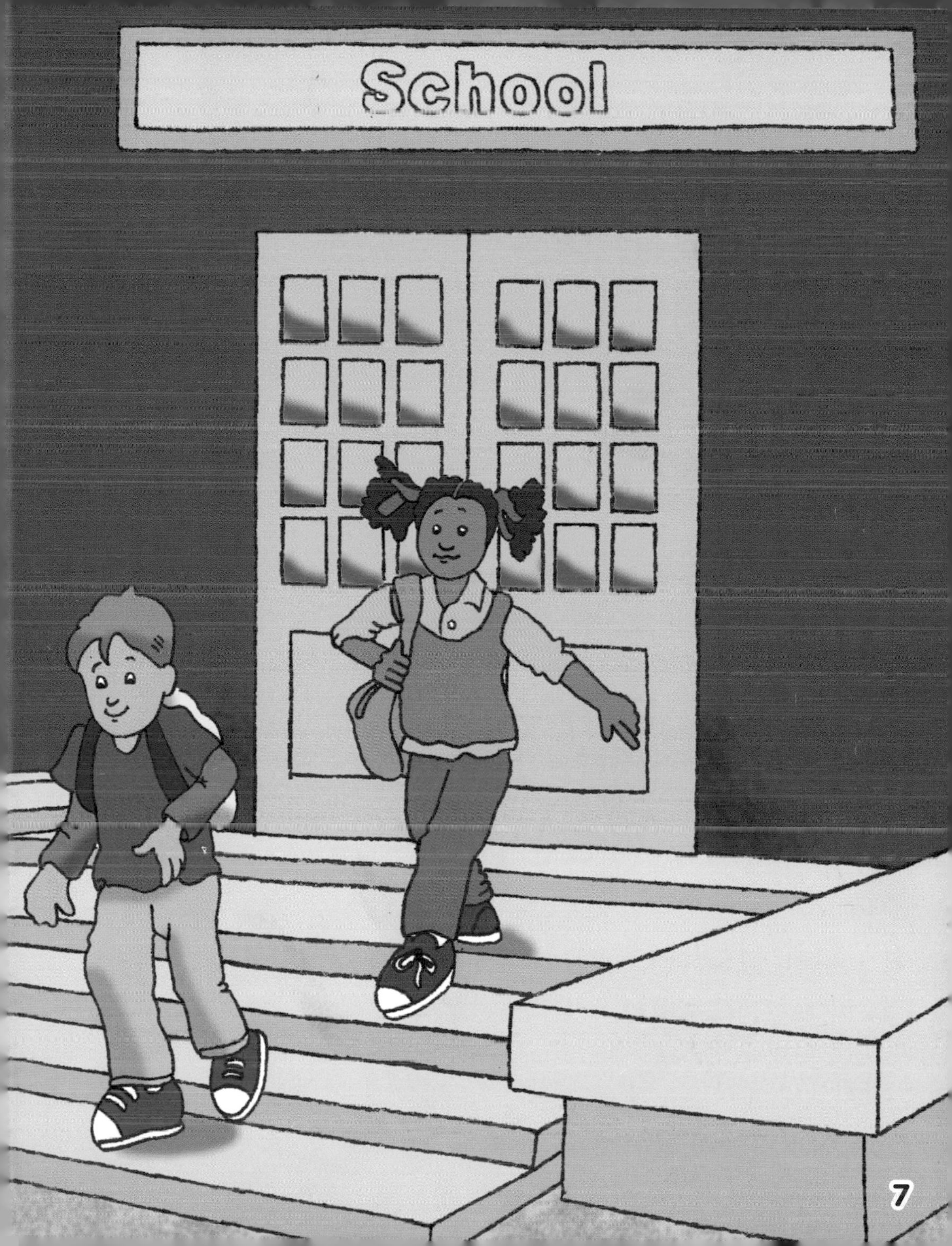
School

Look up there.
Look way, way up.
How pretty the sky is.
So blue. So blue.

Oh, look at that.
Look at them go.
Away, away, away.

And look down here.
See what is down here.
Down, down, down.
Red, yellow, and brown.

I will get something for work.
I will work and work.
Then we can have fun.

Now see what we can do.
We can play and have fun.
Jump, jump, jump.

Mother! Mother!

Yes, I see you but I want you
to come with me.
Get in the car.

I like it here.
Look at this.

Look at this apple.
It is red and good to eat.

18

Look at this—
and this—
and this.

Oh, Mother.
Will you get one for me?
I like this one.

Yes, yes.
This is a good one.

Father. Father.
Look what I have.
Will you help with it?

23

Yes, yes.
We can make something funny.
Look at this.

Oh, oh, oh.

Look at the moon.
So big. So big.
So yellow and pretty.

Here you are with me.
And here I am with you.
Oh, how good it is to
have a friend, dear dragon.

The following activities support the findings of the National Reading Panel that determined the most effective components for reading instruction are: Phonemic Awareness, Phonics, Vocabulary, Fluency, and Text Comprehension.

Phonemic Awareness: The /f/ and /v/ sounds

1. Say the word fan and ask your child to repeat the /**f**/ sound.

2. Say the word van and ask your child to repeat the /**v**/ sound.

3. Explain to your child that you are going to say some words and you would like her/him to show you one finger if the sound in the word is /**f**/, as in fan or two fingers if the sound in the word is /**v**/, as in van.

face	vase	far	fork	vest
beef	move	leave	vent	fox
vine	vote	fast	elf	have
dive	fish	very	view	food
fun	love	leaf	roof	

Phonics: Consonants f and v

1. Demonstrate how to form the letters **f** and **v** for your child.

2. Have your child practice writing **f** and **v** at least three times each.

3. Divide a piece of paper in half by folding it the long way. Draw a line on the fold. Turn it so that the paper has two columns. Write the words fan and van at the top of the columns.

4. Write the words above on separate index cards. Ask your child to sort the words based on the **f** and **v** spellings.

Word Work: Plurals

1. Explain to your child that when there is more than one of something it is

a plural (for example boy/boys, girl/girls, cloud/clouds, etc.).

2. Explain to your child that when words end in the /**f**/ sound, and it is plural, the /**f**/ sound becomes the /**v**/ sound and **es** is added.

3. Write the following words in a list: leaf, elf, knife, life, loaf, scarf, wife, wolf.

4. Spell the word leaves next to the word leaf to demonstrate.

5. Ask your child to change the rest of the words to plurals (elves, knives, lives, loaves, scarves, wives, wolves).

Fluency: Echo Reading

1. Reread the story to your child at least two more times while your child tracks the print by running a finger under the words as they are read. Ask your child to read the words he or she knows with you.

2. Reread the story, stopping after each sentence or page to allow your child to read (echo) what you have read. Repeat echo reading and let your child take the lead.

Text Comprehension: Discussion Time

1. Ask your child to retell the sequence of events in the story.

2. To check comprehension, ask your child the following questions:

   • What happened to the leaves on the trees?

   • Why were the geese flying away?

   • Who helped the boy carve the pumpkin? Why did he need help?

   • What do you like to do in fall? Why?

WORD LIST

It's Fall, Dear Dragon **uses the 75 words listed below.**
This list can be used to practice reading the words that appear in the text.
You may wish to write the words on index cards and use them to help your
child build automatic word recognition. Regular practice with these words
will enhance your child's fluency in reading connected text.

a	dear	here	oh	then
am	do	how	one	there
and	down		out	this
apple	dragon	I		to
are		in	play	
at	eat	is	pretty	up
away		it		
	Father		red	want
be	for	jump	run	way
big	friend(s)			we
blue	fun	like	school	what
brown	funny	look	see	will
but			sky	with
	get	make	so	work
can	go	me	something	
cannot	good	moon		yellow
car		Mother	that	yes
come	have		the	you
	help	now	them	

ABOUT THE AUTHOR Margaret Hillert has written over 80 books for
children who are just learning to read. Her books
have been translated into many different languages and over a million children
throughout the world have read her books. She first started writing poetry as
a child and has continued to write for children and adults throughout her life. A
first grade teacher for 34 years, Margaret is now retired from teaching and lives in
Michigan where she likes to write, take walks in the morning, and care for her three cats.

Photograph by Glenna Washburn

ABOUT THE ADVISER Shannon Cannon contributed the activities pages that appear in
this book. Shannon serves as a literacy consultant and provides
staff development to help improve reading instruction. She is a frequent presenter at educational
conferences and workshops. Prior to this she worked as an elementary school teacher and as
president of a curriculum publishing company.